A. Mary F. Robinson

Songs, Ballads, and a Garden Play

A. Mary F. Robinson

Songs, Ballads, and a Garden Play

ISBN/EAN: 9783744770439

Printed in Europe, USA, Canada, Australia, Japan

Cover: Foto ©Andreas Hilbeck / pixelio.de

More available books at **www.hansebooks.com**

SONGS, BALLADS,

AND

A GARDEN PLAY

-

BY

A. MARY F. ROBINSON

LONDON
T. FISHER UNWIN
—
1888

41097

DEDICATION.

———————

DEAR MABEL,—*A long while ago, when we had the courage of youth and our opinions, you once confided to me that you had no quarrel against poetry, for a change, "when it was short and had a tale in it."   In this little book I think all the pieces are short, or else they are a story; and so, dear Novelist (in memory of the days when you meant to be nearly everything else under the sun, but never a novelist), take this book, which may remind you that even then you liked a tale.*

Ah, but your tales are of a different order.   You are a Realist; and how shall I recommend to you these superficial and fantastic ballads, which only pretend to be adventures, except when they are allegories?—and that alternative, I fear, will scarcely recommend them.   Shall I tell you that they are founded upon fact?   That Kung von der Rosen, Mary Harcourt, Saint Elizabeth and Joan of Arc really lived and underwent, more or less, these adventures?   Shall I tell you that the Legends of Servia still preserve a sort of warrant for the story of St. Maur?   That I, too, have my documents and my authorities ; a line of Shahied the Bactrian in the Stars ; a verse of the quaint " Ballade du Christ" in the last of my ballads ; and that a well-known passage of M. Renan's suggested the Antiphon which will seem so faint and weak to you ? But in the act of making it, I forego this apology, perceiving that upon all this solid foundation I have only raised a bubble of subjective verse—while you, happy creature, out of an airy image conjure a reality that mocks this phantasmal world in which we move.

So I will give you the book merely because you liked the " Tower of St. Maur "—you, first critic, earliest audience, of so many of my verses—and because the little Garden Play may recall to you one happy afternoon, more than a year ago, when Vernon and you and I walked up and down the sunny Epsom garden and laid a deep plan for the acting of that trifle.   The only real things, you know, are the things that never happen ; and so it will always seem to me that the Play belongs to you and Vernon and to the Epsom garden.

TORQUAY, *Feb.* 27, 1888.

CONTENTS.

———✦———

SONGS OF THE INNER LIFE.

8   *CONTENTS.*

SONGS OF THE INNER LIFE (continued).

SPRING SONGS.

ROMANTIC BALLADS.

OUR LADY OF THE BROKEN HEART.

Songs of the Inner Life.

Toda la vida es sueño
Y los sueños sueño son.

ὄναρ ἡμερόφαντον ἀλαίνει.

Eschylus.

ETRUSCAN TOMBS.

I.

To think the face we love shall ever die,
  And be the indifferent earth, and know us
    not !
To think that one of us shall live to cry
  On one long buried in a distant spot !

O wise Etruscans, faded in the night   [trace,
  Yourselves, with scarce a rose-leaf on your
You kept the ashes of the dead in sight,
  And shaped the vase to seem the vanished
    face.

But, O my Love, my life is such an urn
  That tender memories mould with constant
    touch,
Until the dust and earth of it they turn
  To your dear image that I love so much :

A sacred urn, filled with the sacred past,
That shall recall you while the clay shall last.

II.

These cinerary urns with human head
  And human arms that dangle at their sides,
The earliest potters made them or their dead,
  To keep the mother's ashes or the bride's.

O rude attempt of some long-spent despair—
  With symbol and with emblem discontent—
To keep the dead alive and as they were,
  The actual features and the glance that
    went !

The anguish of your art was not in vain,
  For lo, upon these alien shelves removed
The sad immortal images remain,
  And show that once they lived and once
    you loved.

But oh, when I am dead may none for me
Invoke so drear an immortality !

III.

Beneath the branches of the olive yard
  Are roots where cyclamen and violet grow ;
Beneath the roots the earth is deep and hard,
  And there a king was buried long ago.

The peasants digging deeply in the mould
  Cast up the autumn soil about the place,
And saw a gleam of unexpected gold,
  And underneath the earth a living face.

With sleeping lids and rosy lips he lay
  Among the wreaths and gems that mark the
    king
One moment ; then a little dust and clay
  Fell shrivelled over wreath and urn and
    ring.

A carven slab recalls his name and deeds,
Writ in a language no man living reads.

IV.

Here lies the tablet graven in the past,
  Clear-charactered and firm and fresh of line.
See, not a word is gone; and yet how fast
  The secret no man living may divine!

What did he choose for witness in the grave?
  A record of his glory on the earth?
The wail of friends? The Pæans of the
    brave?
  The sacred promise of the second birth?

The tombs of ancient Greeks in Sicily
  Are sown with slender discs of graven
      gold
Filled with the praise of Death: "Thrice
      happy he
  Wrapt in the milk-soft sleep of dreams
      untold!"

They sleep their patient sleep in altered
    lands,
The golden promise in their fleshless hands.

ADAM AND EVE.

WHEN Adam fell asleep in Paradise
    He made himself a helpmeet as he dreamed ;
And, lo ! she stood before his waking eyes,
    And was the woman that his vision seemed.

She knelt beside him there in tender awe
    To find the living fountain of her soul,
And so in either's eyes the other saw
    The light they missed in Heaven, and knew
        the goal.

Thrice-blessed Adam, husband of thine Eve !
    She brought thee for her dowry death and
        shame ;
She taught thee one may worship and deceive ;
    But yet thy dream and she were still the
        same ;
Nor ever in the desert turned thine eyes
Towards Lilith by the brooks of Paradise.

2

THE DEPARTURE.

THE night wears on, the lawns are grey with
    dew,
  The Easter of the dawn will soon be here :
And I must leave the happy world I knew,
  And front the Heaven I worship and I fear.

Dawn that in awe and trembling I desire,
  Bloom in the skies as flaming and as bright
As Enoch saw the chariot-wheels of fire
  Divide the darkness of the desert night.

Ah, when beside that palm tree in the sand
  The fiery swiftness trembled, did his will
Grow faint, to leave the long familiar land?
  Or did he feel a dizzie terror still
Lest, like a dream, that chariot should be gone
  And leave him in the wilderness alone ?

ARNOLD VON WINKELRIED.

THE great things that I love I cannot do,
The little things I do I cannot love !
Far from the goal I wander, and above
The voice is mute of Him I never knew.

Nothing is sweet, I find, and nothing true,
And none of all my dreams is dear enough—.
And only one is worth the dreaming of;
If I could give my life and die for you !

O easy death, surrounded with alarms,
Blue ranks of serried spears that swerve and
start
Where heroes clench their eyes and catch
their breath !
To clasp a score of lances in my arms
And from your front to turn them in my heart
And die, and do you service in my death !

NIGHT.

O NIGHT eternal and blue,
   Holy and soft above,
You seem to lay on my forehead
   The touch of an infinite love—

The touch of a love that never
   Will understand me aright—
Why should you touch me and love me,
   O tender and delicate night?

O night look in with your stars
   On the wintry face of despair,
And your stars will eddy and shrivel
   As leaves in a gust of the air.

SPANISH STARS.

(FOR A PICTURE.)

THESE stars that gleam so white and pale
  Through coil on coil of tragic skies
  Are like a serpent's Argus-eyes,
And venomous, and full of bale.

They throb and pulse in all the night,
  Like Life that pulses in a wound,
  Until the unhappy earth has swoon'd
In aching languor out of sight.

O cruel Life ! O gleaming Asp !
  That holds the earth in sick control,
I know thee, Serpent of the Soul,
  And all thy poison well enough,
Who cannot love the thing I clasp,
  Nor ever clasp the thing I love.

TUBEROSES.

I.

THE Tuberose you left me yesterday
    Leans yellowing in the glass we set it in ;
It could not live when you were gone away,
    Poor spike of withering sweetness changed
        and thin.

And all the fragrance of the dying flower
    Is grown too faint and poisoned at the source,
Like passion that survives a guilty hour,
    To find its sweetness heavy with remorse.

What shall we do, my dear, with dying roses?
    Shut them in weighty tomes where none will
        look
—To wonder when the unfrequent page uncloses
    Who shut the wither'd blossoms in the
        book ?—
                         [perish,
What shall we do, my dear, with things that
    Memory, roses, love we feel and cherish ?

II.

Alive and white, we praised the Tuberose,
  So sweet it fill'd the garden with its breath
A spike of waxy bloom that grows and grows
  Until at length it blooms itself to death.

Everything dies that lives—everything dies ;
  How shall we keep the flower we lov'd so
      long ?
O press to death the transient thing we prize,
  Crush it, and shut the elixir in a song.

A song is neither live nor sweet nor white.
  It hath no heavenly blossom tall and pure,
No fragrance can it breathe for our delight,
  It grows not, neither lives ; it may endure.

Sweet Tuberose, adieu ! you fade too fast !
  Only a dream, only a thought, can last.

III.

Who'd stay to muse if Death could never
    wither ?   [pass ?
Who dream a dream if Passion did not
But, once deceived, poor mortals hasten hither
    To watch the world in Fancy's magic glass.

Truly your city, O men, hath no abiding !
    Built on the sand it crumbles, as it must ;
And as you build, above your praise and
    chiding,
    The columns fall to crush you to the dust.

But fashion'd in the mirage of a dream,
    Having nor life nor sense, a bubble of
        nought,
The enchanted City of the Things that seem
    Keeps till the end of time the eternal Thought.

Forswear to-day, forswearing joy and sorrow,
Forswear to-day, O man, and take to-morrow.

LOVE IN THE WORLD.

THE olives where we walk to-day
In the olive-groves are white and grey,
And underneath the shimmering trees
  One almond-bough is faintly pink,
And lilac blow the anemones.

In all the flowers, in all the leaves,
The secret of their pallor heaves :
A tender hint of vanished bliss.
  A rapture just beyond the brink
Of feeling, which we still must miss.

Perhaps when we are dead, my dear,
Our phantoms still shall wander here,
And breathe in this Elysian wood
  (As others breathe for us, I think),
A beauty dimly understood.

A REFLECTION.

THIS song I wrote—ah me, how long ago !
  When up the stair of Heaven and down
    again
  (For even then I did not long remain),
With happy feet I used to come and go.

This ode I sang beneath a laurel-bough
  Where I had sought for Truth among the
    dead ;
  This little verse, and still the page is red,
To soothe some easier pang forgotten now.

I took the dew of lilies grown apart,
  The scanty wine of Amphoras and, bright
And clear, the blood that flows from trivial
    scars.

But with the bitter ink of mine own heart
  I have not written and I must not write,
    Lest rust and acid dim the eternal stars.

HONOUR.

ONE star at least, one star still breaks the
    night,
  Sinister, pallid, as the peace of death.
And, through the rain and wind, a little light
  Streams fitfully across the windy heath.

All round me from the towering seas beneath
  Atlantic billows dash their storms of white,
Among the rocks the angry waters seethe
  Tormented, and my star is out of sight.

Yet shine again, O white Divinity,
  And wheresoe'er thou leadest I will go—
    What, down? Over the cliff's edge?
    Forth and down?

There shines the path I follow! yet I know
  The infamous blind creatures of the sea
    Swim dimly with wide faces where I drown.

GOD IN A HEART.

I.

ONCE, where the unentered Temple stood, at
    noon   [aisle,
  No sun ray pierced the dim unwindowed
And all the flooding whiteness of the moon
  Could only bathe the outer peristyle.

And as we passed we praised the Temple front,
  But one went in ; with careless feet he trod
The long-forgotten pavement moss'd and blunt
  And found the altar of the unprayed-to God.

He reached and lit the tapers of the shrine
  And let their radiance flood the vault ob-
    scure,
But ah ! upon what evil things to shine,
  Blind, crawling, chill, discoloured, and im-
    pure.

And as the Light burns clearer through the
  gloom,   [room.
More foul, more deathly, shows the illumined

II.

O Light of God, lit in the heart of man,
   More welcome than the well in desert sands,
We bless thee fallen hither for a span
   To glorify the Temple made with hands.

We did not dream how foul the Temple was,
   Until thou visitedst the untended shrine :
Thy glory is not peace for us, alas,
   Illumination tragic and divine.

Yet unrelenting pour, revealing Light !
   Scare and annihilate all our blind desires,
Shine through our thoughts, and purify the
     night,
   And burn us clean with thy transcendent
     fires,

Until thou leavest us renewed and whole
Thy mortal Temple of the transient Soul.

HOPE.

(FOR A PICTURE.)

DEAR Angel of the painter, who beheld
  The soul that moves the dusty world we see,
  O clothed-upon with soft humility
Thou patient Hope of kind unvanquished Eld !

Come thou to me, dear Hope, though I be
    held
  Nor good, nor old, nor of thy company ;
  Yet breathe upon mine eyes and let them be
Clear as thine eyes, of every mist dispell'd.

Dear, selfless Hope ! Although thine orb is
    spent,
  The poor grey ashes of a vanish'd star,
    And from the lyre thou bendest o'er are
      gone
    All of the long-worn strings but only one ;
Thou knowest, beyond the broken instrument,
  The Flame, the Music, undisturbed afar.

WRITING HISTORY.

THE profit of my living long ago
  I dedicated to the unloving dead,
Though all my service they shall never know
    Whose world is vanished and their name
      unsaid.

For none remembers now the good, the ill
    They did, the deeds they thought should last
      for aye :
But in the little room my voice can fill
    They shall not be forgotten till I die.

So, in a lonely churchyard by the shore,
    The sea winds drift the sand across the
      mounds
And those forgotten graves are found no more,
    And no man knows the churchyard's holy
      bounds.
                      [hands
Till one come by and stoop with reverent
To clear the graves of their encumbering sands.

THE ALEMBIC.

IN this alembic have I cast my youth,
  For here I do believe if anywhere,
  Here where the fires of death burn all things
    bare
I may distil the eternal gold of Truth.

Therefore the future is an empty name,
  And life to me a dream that will not last,
  And all my care is only for the Past,
Veiled with the veil of no man's ruth or
    shame.

Yea, Death that hast the secret Life withholds,
  Thy meek and patient servitor am I,
    And, from thine alchemy I will not cease
    Until I find amid thine essences,
Writ in a little sand of divers golds,
  The answer to the eternal How and Why.

IN AFFLICTION.

I WATCH the happier people of the house
  Come in and out and talk and go their
    ways ;
I sit and gaze at them ; I cannot rouse
  My heavy mind to share their busy days.

I watch them glide like skaters on a stream
  Across the brilliant surface of the world ;
But I am underneath ; they do not dream
  How deep below the eddying flood is whirl'd.

They cannot come to me, nor I to them ;
  But, if a mightier arm could reach and save,
Should I forget the tide I had to stem ?
  Should I, like these, ignore the abysmal
    wave ?
Yes ! In the radiant air how could I know
How black it is, how fast it is, below ?

3

MELANCHOLIA.

(For an Engraving by Albrecht Dürer.)

So many years I toiled like Caliban
    To fetch the stones and earth to build my
        fane ;
    So many years I thought before the brain
Reluctant would divulge the final plan.

Years upon years to forge the invented tools
    Novel, as all my temple should be new ;
    Years upon years to fashion and to hew
The stones that should astound a world of
        fools.

Now shall I build ? *Cui bono ?*—lo, the salt
    Has lost its savour and I have no will :
What reck I now of gate or dome or vault?

Among the ruins of the thing undone
    I sit and ask myself *Cui bono ?* till
The sun sets, and a bat flies past the sun.

THE WALL.

THE sun falls through the olive-trees
   And shines upon the wall below,
   And lights the wall which cannot know
The Sunlight that it never sees.

I lie and dream ; the Eternal Mind
   Rains down on me and fills me full
   With secrets high and wonderful ;
And still my soul is deaf and blind.

THE IDEA.

BENEATH this world of stars and flowers
  That rolls in visible deity,
I dream another world is ours
  And is the soul of all we see.

It hath no form, it hath no spirit ;
  It is perchance the Eternal Mind ;
Beyond the sense that we inherit
  I feel it dim and undefined.

How far below the depth of being,
  How wide beyond the starry bound ;
It rolls unconscious and unseeing,
  And is as Number or as Sound.

And through the vast fantastic visions
  Of all this actual universe,
It moves unswerved by our decisions,
  And is the play that we rehearse.

THE STARS. [1]

(To J. D.)

SESTINA.

STARS in the sky, fold upon fold of stars !
And still beyond the stars those gulfs of air
Flecked soft and pale with milkier stars be-
    yond,
Millions of miles above our dusky world :
Pale stars, whose light down the unplumbed
    abyss
Falls, ere it reach us, through a thousand
    years.

There was a God in the unwritten years
Who lit the flaming order of the stars :

[1] This piece, Darwinism, and Melancholia, first
appeared in the '' Poésies de Mary Robinson
traduites de l'Anglais par James Darmesteter.''
Paris, Lemerre, 1888.

Let there be Light ! He said, and lo ! the
    abyss
Grew live and tremulous with rustling air,
Grew bright with stars and moons and each a
    world
Shining, a light to other worlds beyond.

O were you even as we, bright orbs beyond
Who shine and shed your glory all these
    years,
Not light, but smoke would fall from every
    world ;
Smoke, black with human evil, black, O stars
With His neglect who lit the sparkling air,
But left within—unformed and void the Abyss.

O stars that dance indifferent in the Abyss,
Our Earth may seem as bright to you beyond ;
Yourselves, to them that breathe your delicate
    air,
As desolate ; Life in the Lunar years
As long : and the straight rivers of the stars
And primal snows divide as drear a world.

And men, perchance, as we, in every world
Fill with their dreams the bright and vast
    abyss :
A Christ has died in vain on all the stars,
And each, unhappy, seeks a star beyond
Where God rewards the dead through endless
    years. . . .
And so we circle, dumb, in the silent air.

What shall we find more holy in all the air?
Lo, when the first, huge, incandescent world
Burst out of Chaos and flamed a million years,
Until, with too much flaming, thro' the abyss
Flake after flake dropped off and flamed be-
    yond :—
That was the God who lit the world of stars !

For Light, the stars ;—for breath, the realms
    of air ;
For Hope, beyond this dark and suffering
    world,
Nought in the Abyss, nor ought in the endless'
    years.

DARWINISM.

WHEN first the unflowering Fern-forest
  Shadowed the dim lagoons of old,
A vague unconscious long unrest
  Swayed the great fronds of green and gold.

Until the flexible stem grew rude,
  The fronds began to branch and bower,
And lo ! upon the unblossoming wood
  There breaks a dawn of apple-flower.

Then on the fruitful Forest-boughs
  For ages long the unquiet ape
Swung happy in his airy house
  And plucked the apple and sucked the grape.

Until in him at length there stirred
  The old, unchanged, remote distress,
That pierced his world of wind and bird
  With some divine unhappiness.

Not Love, nor the wild fruits he sought ;
   Nor the fierce battles of his clan
Could still the unborn and aching thought
   Until the brute became the man.

Long since. . . . And now the same unrest
   Goads to the same invisible goal,
Till some new gift, undreamed, unguessed
   End the new travail of the soul.

ANTIPHON TO THE HOLY SPIRIT.[1]

(Men and Women sing.)

Men.

O THOU that movest all, O Power
 That bringest life where'er Thou art,
O Breath of God in star and flower,
 Mysterious aim of soul and heart ;
Within the thought that cannot grasp Thee
 In its unfathomable hold,
We worship Thee who may not clasp Thee,
 O God, unreckoned and untold !

Women.

O Source and Sea of Love, O Spirit
 That makest every soul akin,
O Comforter whom we inherit,
 We turn and worship Thee within !

[1] M. Ernest Renan in the church at Quimper imagined the men and women of the earth singing a continual Antiphon to the Unknown God.

To give beyond all dreams of giving,
    To lose ourselves as Thou in us,
We long, for Thou, O Fount of living,
    Art lost in Thy creation thus !

Men.

The mass of unborn matter knew Thee,
    And, lo ! the splendid, silent sun
Sprang out to be a witness to Thee
    Who art the All, who art the One ;
The airy plants unseen that flourish
    Their floating strands of filmy rose,
Too small for sight, are Thine to nourish ;
    For Thou art all that breathes and grows.

Women.

Thou art the ripening of the fallows,
    The swelling of the buds in rain ;
Thou art the joy of birth that hallows
    The rending of the flesh in twain ;
O Life, O Love, how undivided
    Thou broodest o'er this world of Thine,
Obscure and strange, yet surely guided
    To reach a distant end divine !

Men.

We know Thee in the doubt and terror
  That reels before the world we see ;
We knew Thee in the faiths of error,
  We know Thee most who most are free.
This phantom of the world around Thee
  Is vast, divine, but not the whole :
We worship Thee, and we have found Thee
  In all that satisfies the soul !

Men and Women.

How shall we serve, how shall we own Thee,
  O Breath of Love and Life and Thought?
How shall we praise, who are not shown Thee?
  How shall we serve, who are as nought ?
Ah, though Thy worlds maintain unbroken
  The silence of their awful round,
A voice within our souls hath spoken,
  And we who seek have more than found.

Spring Songs.

" The earth we pace
Again appears to be
An unsubstantial faery place."

WORDSWORTH.

LA BELLE AU BOIS DORMANT.

DOWN the enchanted Forest grey,
  Hark, a dreamy note is borne !
  'Tis the winding of a horn
Far away !
  Boughs of oak and boughs of thorn
Stir and sway.

        Yet the wood is haunted,
          Silent many a year ;
        Only long-enchanted
          Dreamers linger here.

'Tis a Forest thick and dim,
  Overgrown and hoar indeed,
  Hung with lichen, choked with weed,
To the brim.
  Sleeps the knight and sleeps the steed
Under him.

Here the pale princesses
Lying on the green,
Pillow with their tresses
Their enchanted Queen.

Where the barren branches meet
Still they sleep, and none behold
Robes of dim brocaded gold,
Sandalled feet,
Languid arms and lips a-cold
Pale and sweet.

Here the wind is noiseless,
Here the fountain stops,
Hanging blank and voiceless
Her enchanted drops.

Hark, along the unwonted gale
Rings the winding of a horn ;
Rings thro' all a world forlorn
Glad Reveil.
Till the blossom studs the thorn,
Thick as hail.

Hark the awaken'd thrushes !
Lo ! the deer awake,
Leaping from the rushes,
Through the windy brake.

Till beneath the flowering tree,
Novel music in her ears,
Lo, asleep a thousand years,
It is She !
Blow thy clarion, Spring; she hears !
She is free !

Break, O bower above her,
Briar and thorn divide.
Hark, the Eternal Lover
Calls the Enchanted Bride !

4

SPRING.

SPRING, the tender maiden,
  Like a girl who greets her lover,
Comes, her apron laden
  Deep with leaf and flower we liked of old.
Not a sprig forgetting
  That we then demanded of her,
Changing not nor setting
  Out of place the tiniest frill or fold.

See, the aspen still is
  Hung awry to droop and falter,
Still the leaves of lilies
  Lift aloft their tall and tender sheath.
Wiser than the sages,
  Spring would never dare to alter
What so many ages
  Showed already right in bloom and wreath.

Ah, could Spring remember
  Every thrill and fancy perished
In the soul's December,
  Lost for ever, faded from the truth ;
Holy things and tender,
  Dead, alas, however cherished.
Breathe, O Spring, and render
  That forgotten radiance of our youth !

GOING SOUTH.

A LITTLE grey swallow
    I fled to the vales
    Of the nightingales
And the haunts of Apollo.

Behind me lie the sheer white cliffs, the hollow
    Green waves that break at home, the northern
        gales,
    The oaks above the homesteads in the vales,
For all my home is far, and cannot follow.

O nightingale voices !
    O lemons in flower !
    O branches of laurel !

You all are here, but ah not here my choice is :
    Fain would I pluck one pink-vein'd bloom
        of sorrel,
Or hear the wrens build in some hazel bower.

PROMISE.

UNDER the olives the armour-blue aloes
   Are fountains of colour alive in the grey;
Over the haven a sickle-moon hallows
   The skies of the noon and is dimmer than
      they.

The moon has no ray and the aloe no slender
   Pale spike of a blossom to slant up on high.
(When will you flower, O my Song, in your
   splendour?
   When will you fill with your radiance the
   sky?)

A JINGLE.

BUNCHES of tansy
And violet and pansy
Pluck from the garden to make me a bed.
Carry me slowly,
Lay me there lowly,
Leave me alone with the stars overhead.

Make me a pillow
Of branches of willow
Cover'd with rose-petals softer than down.
Strew me all over
With sweet-smelling clover ;
I shall be dead when the blossoms are brown !

LA CALIFORNIE.

(To E. S.)

AN arid place, I would not call it fair,
　　Low-lying marshes dappled with the sea.
　　A raised white road that reaches endlessly
Across the sunshine in a lilac glare.

One liquid shadow marks the only house,
　　Sunsmitten, white, below the causeway edge,
　　Screen'd from the seawinds with a broken
　　　　hedge
Of straggling cyprus rearing dusty boughs.

Nought else, save only where the wind breaks
　　　　through　　　　　　　　　　　　[plains,
　　Those Indian reeds that end the sun-baked
　　Divides the yellow thicket of the canes,
And dazzles with a sudden breadth of blue.

Sea, marsh, and sun ; and 'tis something less
　　　　than fair.
And yet, my Dear, we were so happy there.

AN ORCHARD AT AVIGNON.

THE hills are white, but not with snow :
 They are as pale in summer time,
For herb or grass may never grow
 Upon their slopes of lime.

Within the circle of the hills
 A ring, all flowering in a round,
An orchard-ring of almond fills
 The plot of stony ground.

More fair than happier trees, I think,
 Grown in well-watered pasture land,
These parched and stunted branches, pink
 Above the stones and sand.

O white, austere, ideal place,
 Where very few will care to come,
Where spring hath lost the waving grace
 She wears for us at home !

Fain would I sit and watch for hours
   The holy whiteness of thy hills,
Their wreath of pale auroral flowers,
   Their peace the silence fills.

A place of secret peace thou art,
   Such peace as in an hour of pain
One moment fills the amazed heart,
   And never comes again.

ROMANTIC BALLADS.

" Old unhappy far-off things,
And battles long ago."

WORDSWORTH.

τί ταῦτα πενθεῖν δεῖ ; παροίχεται πόνος,
παροίχεται δὲ, τοῖσι μὲν τεθνηκόσιν,
τὸ μήποτ᾽ αὖθις μηδ᾽ ἀναστῆναι μέλειν.

ESCHYLUS.

SIR HUGH AND THE SWANS.

(KUNG VON DER ROSEN.   BRUGES, 1488.)

THE wintry nights in Flanders
 Lie thick about the grass ;
We stole between the sentinels,
 They never saw us pass.

The mist was blue on field and fen,
 And ridged the dykes with white ;
The camp-fires of the soldiers
 Burned holes into the night.

They could not see us through the mirk :
 We saw them i' the glow.
A price was on our either head
 And stealthy did we go.

We crept along the inner banks
 Close to the waters grey—
We reached the castle at dawn, the castle
 Where Max in prison lay.

(We blew the golden trumpets all
    For joy, a year agone :
" Long live the King o' the Romans ! "
    The people cried as one.

Now, for the king in prison,
    There's two will dare to die.
There's Hugh o' the Rose, the Jester,
    Sir Hugh o' the Rose, and I.)

We came upon the castle moat
    As the dawn was weak and grey : [Rose,
" There's still an hour," quoth Hugh o' the
    " An hour till break of day.

" Give me the files, the muted files,
    Give me the rope to fling ;
I'll swim to the prison window,
    And hand them to the king.

" I'll swim to the castle and back, Sir John,
    Before the morn is light,
And we'll both lie hid i' the rushes here
    Till we take the boat to-night."

We tied the files, we tied the rope,
  In a little leather sack.
Sir Hugh struck off from the mirky bank,
  The satchel on his back.

I watched him cleave the wan water—
  A bold swimmer was he.
My heart beat high in my bosom,
  For I thought the king was free.

I watched him shoot the middle stream
  And reach the other side—
"Fling up the rope, Sir Hugh o' the Rose"—
  It was the king that cried.

But what's the bird that screeches so shrill?
  What's the whirr and the scream?
The air's astir with dim white wings,
  Like angels in a dream!

The sun uprist beyond the dyke,
  Red in the ghostly air—
'Twas only the swans o' the castle
  Screaming and battling there!

But then I saw them stretch their necks
  And hiss, as traitors do ;
I saw them arch their evil wings
  And strike and stun Sir Hugh.

The king looked out o' the window bars,
  And he was sad belike ;
But I could not see my lord the king
  For the drowned face in the dyke.

The sleepy warders woke and stirred,
  " The swans are mad in the moat ! "
I lifted up Sir Hugh o' the Rose
  And laid him in the boat.

I made him a sark of rushes,
  With stones at the feet and head. . .
In the deepest dyke of Flanders
  Sir Hugh o' the Rose lies dead.

Feb. 2, 1888.

THE TOWER OF ST. MAUR.

"WHERE's my little son, Nourrice,
  And whither is he gone?
The youngest son of all I have,
  He should not gang alone."

"The child is safe enough, lady;
  He's barely gone an hour:
He's gone to see the mason-men,
  Are building at the tower."

"You should have kept him here, Nourrice,
  If I was sleeping then—
He's over young to gang alone
  Among the mason-men."

"Lie still, lie still, my sweet lady,
  There's nought to sorrow for;
The child is safe enough, I think,
  I' the keeping of St. Maur!"

5

An hour's gone by, an hour or two,
   And still they're out-of-door —
" I wish they'd come at last, Nourrice,
   My heart is sick and sore."

" Now hush, lady, my sweet lady,
   The moon's still small and young ;
If they're home before the curfew bell
   They'll not ha' stayed too long."

St. Maur has ta'en his youngest son,
   To the riverside they're gone,
To see the busy mason-men
   Building a tower of stone.

" O why do they build the tower so strong
   Against the riverside ?
I never saw the wall, father,
   That was so strong and wide."

" God knows the tower had need be strong
   Between my foes and thee ?
Should once Lord Armour enter, child,
   An ill death would ye dee."

" We need not fear Lord Armour, father,
    Nor any of his kin ;
Since God has given us such a wall,
    They cannot enter in."

"O twice, my babe, and thrice, my babe,
    Ere ever that I was born,
Lord Armour's men have entered in
    Betwixt the night and the morn.

" And once I found my nurse's room
    Was red with bloody men . . .
I would not have thy mother die
    As died my mother then.

" And 'tis not seven nights ago,
    I heard, clear in a dream,
The bugle cry of Armour,
    Shrill over wood and stream."

" But if so foul a raid, father,
    Fell out so long agone,
Why did they never build before
    A wall and tower of stone?"

" Many's the time, my pretty babe,
　　Ere ever this way you went,
We built the tower both thick and broad—
　　An' we might as well ha' stent.

" Many's the time we built the tower,
　　Wi' the grey stone and the brown.
But aye the floods in autumn
　　Washed all the building down.

" And in my mind I see the morn
　　When we'll be brought to dee—
Yoursel' and your seven brothers,
　　And your young mother, and me.

"And oh, were it any but Armour,
　　Oh God, were it any but she—
Before the Lord, my eyes grow dark
　　With the ill sight that I see."

Among the busy mason-men,
　　Are building at the tower,
There's a swarthy gipsy mason,
　　A lean man and a dour.

He's lain the hammer down at last
   Out of his bony hand . . .
" Did ye never hear the spell, St Maur,
   Gars any tower to stand ? "

" O what's the spell, thou black gipsy,
   I prithee rede it now :
There never was any mason-man
   Shall earn such wage as thou."

" I dare not speak the spell, St. Maur,
   Lest you should do me an ill,
For a cruel spell, and an evil spell,
   Is the spell that works your will."

" There's no spell but I'll risk it, man,
   An' the price were half my lands—
To keep my wife and children safe
   Out of Lord Armour's hands."

" O, more than lands, and more than fee,
   You'll pay me for the spell——" [blood,
" An' the price were half my heart's red
   I'd pay it down as well."

"O what's the blood of a sinful heart
  To bind the stones that fall?
St. Maur, you'll build your christened child
  Alive into the wall."

St. Maur has turned on his heel so light,
  And angry he turns away :
"Gang to the devil another time
  When ye ask what ye ask to-day."

He's ta'en his young son by the hand—
  He's opened wide the gate,
"Your mother's been sick a month by now,
  And she'll mourn sore if we're late."

They had not gone a little way,
  An' the child began to call—
"See how the flood runs high, father,
  And washes at the wall !"

They had not gone a mickle way,
  St. Maur began to brood,
"'Tis the bugle cry of Armour,
  Shrill over stream and wood."

" And must they slay me, father dear,
    And my seven brothers tall ? "
" Gin that's the blast of Armour, laddie,
    I fear they'll slay us all."

" And will they slay my mother, then,
    That looks so bonny and small ?"
"Come back, come back, thou little lad
    To the masons at the wall."

The flood runs high and still more high,
    And washes stone from stone—
" In another hour," say the masons,
    " Our work is all undone."

The flood runs high and still more high,
    And the bugle rings anear ;
The masons looking o'er the wall
    Are blue and stark with fear.

There's one that's neither stark nor wan,
    But never he looked so well ;   [cries,
" Shall I gang to the devil, St. Maur ? " he
    " Or say, shall I gang to yoursel' ?"

He's set the child high in the air
  Upon his shoulder bone ;
" Shall I leave them all for Armour,
  Or shall I take but one ? "

Never an answer spake St. Maur,
  And never a word he said :
There was not one o' the mason men
  Looked half so wan and dead.

The gipsy's ta'en the frighted child
  And set him in the wall :
" There's a bonny game to play, little man,
  The bonniest game of all.

" You'll stand so still and stark, my lad ;
  I'll build in two's and three's ;
And I'll throw you a red, red apple in,
  When the stones reach to your knees.

" You'll stand so still and stark, my lad ;
  I'll lay the stones in haste ;
And I'll throw you the forester's whistle
  When they reach above your waist.

" You'll stand so still and stark, my lad,
   You'll watch the stones that rise ;
And I'll throw you in your father's sword,
   When they reach above your eyes.

" And if you tire o' the play, my lad,
   You've but to raise a shout :
At the least word o' your father's mouth,
   I'll stop and pluck you out."

The gipsy-man builds quick and light,
   As if he played a play,
And the child laughs with a frighted laugh,
   And the tower ceases to sway.

St. Maur stares out of his bloodshot eyes,
   Like one that's well nigh mad ;   [high
The tower stands fast, and the stones rise
   About the little lad.

" O father, father, lift me out !
   The stones reach over my eyes,
And I cannot see you now, father,
   So swift the walls uprise.

"O father, lift me out, father !
  I cannot breathe at all,
For the stones reach up beyond my head,
  And its dark down i' the wall."

But never an answer spake St. Maur,
  Never a word but one :   [mason,
"Have you finished your devil's work,
  Or when will the deed be done?"

"Oh, the work is done that ye wished, St.
    Maur,
  'Twill last for many a year ;
There's scarce a sound in the wall by now
  A mother might not hear.

"Gang home, gang home in peace, St. Maur,
  And sleep sound if you can ;
There's never a flood shall rock this tower,
  And never a mortal man.

"Gang home and kiss your bonny wife,
  And bid her mourn and fast . .
She'll weep a year for her youngest child,
  But she'll dry her eyes at last.

"You'll say he fell in the flood, St. Maur,
　　But you'll not deceive yoursel',
For you've lost the bonniest thing you had,
　　And you'll remember well.

"Your wife will mourn him a year, St.
　　Maur,
　　You'll mourn him all your life,
For you've lost the bonniest thing you had,
　　Better than bairns or wife."

Feb. 8, 1888.

THE DUKE OF GUELDRES'
WEDDING.

GUELDRES, A.D., 1405.

THE Queen and all her waiting-maids
  Are playing at the ball;
Mary Harcourt, the King's cousin,
  Is fairest of them all.

The Queen and all her waiting-maids
  Are out on Paris Green;
Mary Harcourt, the King's cousin,
  Is fairer than the Queen.

The King sits in his council room,
  The grey lords at his side;
And through the open window-pane,
  He sees the game outside.

The King sits in the Council-room,
　The young lords at his feet ;
And through the pane he sees the ball,
　And the ladies young and fleet.

" O bonny Mary Harcourt
　Is seventeen to-day ;
'Tis time a lover courted her,
　And carried her away.

" Where shall I give my own cousin ?
　Where shall I give my kin ?
And who shall be the peer of France
　Her lily hand to win ? "

Then up and spake an old grey lord,
　And keen, keen was his eye :
" Your friends ye have already, Sire,
　Your foes ye'll have to buy."

Then up and spake that old grey lord,
　And keen, keen was his glance :
" Marry the girl to Gueldres, Sire,
　And gain a friend to France ! "

" O how shall I wed my own cousin
    To a little Flemish Lord ? "
" Nay ; Gueldres is a gallant Duke,
    And girt with many a sword. "

" What will the Duke of Limburg say
    If such a deed be done ? "   [lord,
" Last night your foes were twain, my
    To-day there'll be but one ! "

" Yet Limburg is a jealous man,
    And Gueldre's quick and wroth ! "
" To-morrow they'll hew each other
      down,
    And you'll be quit of both ! "

O blithe was Mary Harcourt,
    The blithest of them all ;   [lord,
When forth there stepped that old grey
    Out of the Council-hall.

O sad was Mary Harcourt,
    And sorry was her face,   [lord,
When back there stepped that old grey
    And left her in her place.

" O shall I leave my own country,
    And shall I leave my kin?"
O strange will be the Flemish streets
    My feet shall wander in !

" O shall I learn to brace a sword,
    And brighten up a lance?
I've learned to pull the flowers all day,
    All night I've learned to dance !

"O shall I marry a Flemish knight,
    And learn a Flemish tongue?
Would I had died an hour ago,
    When I was blithe and young?"

Twice the moon and thrice the moon
    Has waxed and waned away,
And all the streets of Gueldres shine
    With sammet and with say;

And out of every window hang
    The crimson squares of silk;
The fountains run with claret wine,
    The runnels flow with milk.

The ladies and the knights of France,
How gallantly they ride !
But all in silk and red roses,
The fairest is the Bride.

" O welcome Mary Harcourt,
Thrice welcome lady mine ;
There's not a knight in all the world
Shall be so true as thine.

" There's venison in the aumbry, Mary,
There's claret in the vat ;
Come in and breakfast in the hall
Where once my mother sat."

O red, red is the wine that flows,
And sweet the minstrels play ;
But white is Mary Harcourt
Upon her wedding-day.

O merry are the wedding-guests
That sit on either side ;
But pale below her crimson flowers,
And homesick is the Bride.

They had not filled or drank a cup,
   A cup but barely three,
When the Duke of Limburg's herald
   Came riding furiously.

They had not filled or drank a cup,
   A cup but barely four,
When the Duke of Limburg's herald
   Came riding to the door.

" O where's the Duke of Gueldre-land,
   O where's the groom so gay ?
My master sends a wedding-glove
   To grace the wedding-day !

" O where's the Duke of Gueldre-land,
   And where's the bride so sweet ?
That I may lift this iron glove
   And hurl it to their feet.

" To-day you drink the wine, Gueldres,
   Your true-love at your side ;
You'll lie in the grave to-morrow night,
   And Limburg with the bride ! "

Gueldres is a gallant knight,
   Gallant and good to see ;
So swift he bends to raise the glove,
   Lifting it courteously.

His coat is of the white velvet,
   His cap is of the black,
A cloak of gold and silver work
   Hangs streaming at his back.

He's ta'en the cloak from his shoulders,
   As gallant as may be :
" Take this, take this, Sir Messenger,
   You've ridden far for me !

" And welcome, welcome, is your glove,
   And welcome is your word ;
Bright are my lady's bonny eyes,
   And brighter is the sword.

" Now speed you back to Limburg
   As quickly as you may,
I'll meet your lord to-morrow morn,
   To-day's my wedding-day."

The morrow Mary Harcourt
  Is standing at the door :
" I let him go with an angry word,
  And I'll see him never more.

" Mickle I wept to leave my kin,
  Mickle I wept to stay
Alone in foreign Gueldres, when
  My ladies rode away.

" With tears I wet my wedding-sheets,
  That were so fine and white—
But for one glint of your eye, Gueldres,
  I'd give my soul to-night ! "

O long waits Mary Harcourt,
  Until the sun is down ;
The mist creeps up along the street,
  And darkens all the town.

O long waits Mary Harcourt,
  Till grey the dawn up springs ;
But who is this that rides so fast
  That all the pavement rings ?

" Is that yourself in the dawn, Gueldres ?
　Or is it your ghost so wan?"
" O hush ye, hush ye, my bonny bride,
　'T is I, a living man.

" There's blood upon my hands, Mary,
　There's blood upon my lance ;
Go in, and leave a rougher knight
　Than e'er you met in France ! "

" O what's the blood of a foe, Gueldres,
　That I should keep away?
I did not love you yester morn,
　I'd die for you to-day.

" I'll hold your dripping horse, Gueldres,
　I'll hold your heavy lance ;
I'd rather die your serving-maid
　Than live the Queen of France ! "

He's caught her in his happy arms,
　He's clasped her to his side.
May God give every gallant knight
　So blithe and bonny a bride !
April 27, 1887.

RUDEL AND THE LADY OF
TRIPOLI.

(PROVENCE, 1150.)

THERE was in all the world of France
  No singer half so sweet :
The first note of his viol brought
  A crowd into the street.

He stepped as young and bright and glad
  As the Angel Gabriel ;
And only when we heard him sing
  Our eyes forgot Rudel.

And as he sat in Avignon
  With princes at their wine,
In all that lusty company
  Was none so fresh and fine.

His kirtle's of the Arras-blue,
　His cap of pearls and green,
His golden curls fall tumbling round
　The fairest face I've seen.

But hark ! the lords are laughing loud
　And lusty in their mirth,
For each has pledged his own lady,
　The fairest on the earth.

" Now, hey, Rudel !   You singer, Rudel !
　Say, who's the fairest lass ?
I'll wager many a lady's eyes
　Have been your looking-glass ! "

And loud the silver goblets rang,
　And clattered chain and sword,
His lady's portrait each has ta'en,
　And dashed it on the board.

Then half he smiled and half he sighed,
　His laughing eye was blurred ;
He took the pictures in his hand,
　Nor ever spake a word.

For in the woods of Tarascon,
  Where grey the olives bow,
There dwelt a slender maiden,
  Whom he remembered now.

O painted eyes and painted locks,
  And look of dainty wile ;
He lifts them up and lays them down
  With that remembering smile.

O frame of gold and frame of pearls,
  Ivory carven and cleft ;
He lifts them up and lays them down
  Till only one is left.

There's only a twist of silver
  About a parchment skin
That's lain so close against a heart
  The colour's worn and thin.

There's only a twist of foreign wire—
  There's only a faded face—
What ails, what ails Geoffrey Rudel ?
  He 's fallen from his place.

He's fallen plumb across the board
  Without a word or sign ;
The golden curls that hide his face
  Are dappled in the wine.

He's fallen numb and dumb as death,
  While all the princes stare—
Then up one old Crusading Knight
  Arose, and touched his hair :

" Rudel, Rudel, Geoffrey Rudel,
  Give me the picture back !
Without her face against my breast
  The world grows dim and black.

" Rudel, Rudel, Geoffrey Rudel,
  Give back my life to me !
Or I will kill you where you lie,
  And take it desperately !"

Then straight awoke and rose Rudel—
  And hey, but he was white,
And thin and fierce his lips were set ;
  His eyes were cold and bright.

The picture's in his left hand,
   The dagger's in the right.
Stabbed to the core, upon the floor
   Fell down that stranger-knight.

Rang loud the swords in the scabbards,
   The voices loud and high—
"Let pass, let pass!" cried out Rudel,
   "Let pass before he die—"

The lords fell back in grim array
   Around the dying man :
"For pity and pardon let him kneel
   And pray, if so he can!"

But never a word said Geoffrey
   Save only, "Who is she?"
One moment smiled the dying man—
   "The Lady of Tripoli!"

He opened wide his sea-blue eyes,
   Dead, in a face of stone. . . .
Out to the windy dark Rudel,
   Unhindered, rushed alone.

PART II.

ALONE, alone, goes young Rudel
  Beside the unflowering sea—
The stars begin to point the blue,
  And still alone is he.

In vain for him the minstrels pipe,
  And all in vain for him
The ladies dance by candle-light
  Until the dawn is dim.

In vain for him the huntsmen blow
  Their revels on the horn,
The hunters dash across the sands
  Unnoticed in the morn.

He's gone to seek the dreary moor,
  Where no man lives or stirs,
Only the wheeling moor-fowl
  That rise out of the furze.

He's gone to seek the lonely tarns
  That nothing earthly fills,
Only the rains of Heaven
  That fall upon the hills.

And none above the Cyprus wine
  Can chaunt a roundelay,
And boast, while others stoop to hear,
  " Rudel's new song to-day ! "

For silent is the ballad now,
  And silent is the song,
And all alone above the sea
  He wanders all day long.

At noon, when heathen pilgrims pray
  About her Eastern place,
He draws the parchment from his breast
  And gazes on her face.

Then in his gaunt and hollow eyes
  A tender smile will spring,
Like the first faint flush of almond bloom
  On leafless woods in spring.

And humbled to the very heart,
   He looks across the sea,
And images beyond the waves
   The domes of Tripoli.
" And who am I," he grieves, " alas,
   To sing of such as she ! "

And so, and even so for years,
   For years and every day,
Like pilgrims to the Holy Land,
   He wears his life away.

Faded with all the rains of Heaven,
   His tattered cloak of green;
And torn his locks, and dark his brow,
   And altered is his mien.

And none of all his friends of old
   Who praised and loved him well,
Would turn to meet this ragged man
   And laugh, and cry " Rudel ! "

PART III.

" HEW the timbers of sandalwood,
    And planks of ivory ;
Rear up the shining masts of gold,
    And let us put to sea.

" Sew the sails with a silken thread
    That all are silken too,
Sew them with scarlet pomegranates,
    Upon a sheet of blue.

" Rig the ship with a rope of gold,
    And let us put to sea—
And now good-bye to good Marseilles,
    And hey for Tripoli ! "

All the harbour's full of boats,
    A crowd is on the strand,
" Adieu, Rudel ! adieu, Rudel ! "
    Comes echoing from the land.

" Why did you leave us, dear Rudel,
  To roam for seven year—
And come and sing one golden song
  And go and leave us here ?

" Why did you ever hush so long,
  If you can sing so well?
A song ! one other perfect song !
  One other song, Rudel ! "

Up and down the golden ship
  That's sailing to the south,
Rudel goes singing to himself,
  A smile about his mouth.

And up the masts and on the bridge
  The sailors stop to hear :
There's not a lark in the May-heaven
  Can sing so high and clear !

There's not a thrush or a nightingale
  Can sing so full and glad.
Yet there's the sigh of a soul in the song,
  And the soul is wise and sad.

Rudel goes singing to himself
  As he looks across the sea—
" Lady," he says, " I'll sing at last,
  Please God, in Tripoli."

For pale across the wan water
  A shining wonder grows,
As pale as on the murky night
  The dawn of grey and rose.

And dim across the flood so grey
  A city 'gins to rise,
A pale, enchanted Eastern place,
  White under radiant skies.

O domes and spires, O minarets,
  O heavy-headed drowse
Of nodding palms, O strangling rose
  Sweet in the cypress boughs !

" Heave-to, O mariners, heave ashore
  As swiftly as may be.
Go, now, my stripling page, along
  The streets of Tripoli,

And say Rudel, Rudel, has come,
    And say that I am he."

The page-boy runs along the streets,
    The mariners gear the ship ;
Rudel sits down at a gold tressel,
    A wine cup at his lip.

"And when, and when, O when," he cries,
    "Shall I see my heart's delight ? "
And lo, there glides along the quay
    A lady like a light.

"And when, O Mary in Heaven ! " he cries,
    "Shall I hear her speak my name?"
And lo, there moves towards the ship
    A lady like a flame.

You could not tell how tall she was,
    So heaved the light and fell :
The shining of enchanted gems,
    The waving of a veil,
She drifts across the golden deck,
    And stands before Rudel.

But, as she bends to clasp Rudel,
  He sees her snow-white hair
Ravelled in many a ring about
  Her shoulders gaunt and bare.

And as she bends to kiss Rudel
  He meets her gleaming eyes,
That glitter in her ancient skin
  Like Fire that never dies.

And as she calls his name aloud,
  Her voice is thin and strange,
As night-winds in the standing reeds
  When the moon's about to change.

She's opened wide her bridal arms,
  She's bent her wintry face ;—
What ails, what ails Geoffrey Rudel?
  He has fallen from his place.

He's fallen plumb across the board
  Without a word or sign,
His golden locks that stream so bright,
  Are dappled in the wine.

7

He's fallen from her straining arms
  Dead as the senseless stone . . .
Out of the world, into the dark,
  His spirit flits alone,

April 24, 1887.

A BALLAD OF ORLEANS.

1429.

THE fray began at the middle-gate,
   Between the night and the day;
Before the matin bell was rung
   The foe was far away.
There was no knight in the land of France
   Could gar that foe to flee,
Till up there rose a young maiden,
   And drove them to the sea.

   Sixty forts around Orleans town,
      And sixty forts of stone!
   Sixty forts at our gates last night—
      To-day there is not one!

Talbot, Suffolk, and Pole are fled
   Beyond the Loire, in fear—
Many a captain who would not drink,
   Hath drunken deeply there—

Many a captain is fallen and drowned,
  And many a knight is dead,
And many die in the misty dawn
  While the forts are burning red.

  Sixty forts around Orleans town,
    And sixty forts of stone !
  Sixty forts at our gates last night—
    To-day there is not one !

The blood ran off our spears all night
  As the rain runs off the roofs—
God rest their souls that fell i' the fight
  Among our horses' hoofs !
They came to rob us of our own
  With sword and spear and lance,
They fell and clutched the stubborn earth,
  And bit the dust of France !

  Sixty forts around Orleans town,
    And sixty forts of stone !
  Sixty forts at our gates last night—
    To-day there is not one .

We fought across the moonless dark
  Against their unseen hands—
A knight came out of Paradise
  And fought among our bands.
Fight on, O maiden knight of God,
  Fight on and do not tire—
For lo ! the misty break o' the day
  Sees all their forts on fire !

    Sixty forts around Orleans town,
      And sixty forts of stone !
    Sixty forts at our gates last night—
      To-day there is not one !

1886.

THE DEAD MOTHER.

(NORTHUMBERLAND, A.D. 1290.)

LORD ROLAND on his roan horse
    Is riding far and fast,
Though white the eddying snow is driven
    Along the northern blast.

There's snow upon the holly-bush,
    There's snow upon the pine,
There's many a bough beneath the snow
    He had not thought so fine—
For last time Roland crossed the moor
    He rode to Palestine.

Now pale across the windy hills
    A castle 'gins to rise,
With unsubstantial turrets thin,
    Against the windy skies.

" Welcome, O welcome, Towers of Sands,
  I welcome you again !
Yet often in my Syrian tent
  I saw you far more plain."

Lord Roland spurs his roan horse
  Through all the snow and wind—
And soon he's reached those towers so gray,
  And left the moor behind.

" Welcome, Sir John the Steward !
  How oft in Eastern lands
I've called to mind your English face,
  And sighed to think of Sands.

" If still you love your old play-mate
  You loved so well of yore—
Go up and tell my mother now
  That Roland's at the door."

"O how shall I tell you, Lord Roland,
  The news that you must know ?—
Your mother is dead, Lord Roland—
  She died a month ago."

About the middle of the night,
  When all things turn to sleep,
Lord Roland in the darkness
  Learned that a man can weep.

" O why did I stay so long away,
  And tarry so many a year—
And now your face I cannot see,
  Your voice I cannot hear.

" In the battle-ranks of Palestine
  I saw you clear and plain;
But now I sob and stretch mine arms
  And close mine eyes in vain.

" There's a flood of death between us now
  And its waves are dark and dour,
But if my voice can reach across,
  And if the dead have power,
Come back, come back from Heaven,
    mother,
  An' it be but for an hour ! "

It's a long, long road from Heaven to Earth,
   And a weary road, I ween,
For them that passed the Gates of Death
   To reach those gardens green ;

It's a long road from the heart of the grave,
   To the home where kinsmen sleep—
But a mother thinks no road is long,
   That hears her children weep.

The wind has dropt behind the moor,
   The night is quiet and still,
What makes the flesh of Lord Roland
   To shudder and turn chill?

A breeze blows in at the door, so white,
   And the fire burns sullen and red,
And out of the wind he hears a voice,
   And he knows the voice is dead.

And something stirs in the firelight,
   Drifting nigher and nigher—
" My hands are blue," says the pale voice,
   " I'll warm them at the fire."

Lord Roland stares across the dusk
　With stern and terrible eyes,
But there's only a wind in the firelight,
　A wind that shudders and sighs.

" My limbs are faint," sighs the weary voice,
　" My feet are bruised and torn—
It's long I've seen no linen sheets,
　I'll rest me here till morn."

There's a pale shape in the chamber now,
　And shadowy feet that move,
The fire goes out in a sullen ash,
　Like the angry end of love—

And out of doors the red cock cries,
　And then the white and the gray—
Where one spirit crossed Whinny-moor,
　There's two that hurry away.

And still Lord Roland sits alone,
　Stiff, with a look of dread ;
And the cold beams of the morning fall
　About the dead man's head.

　July 5, 1887.

THE KING OF HUNGARY'S DAUGHTER.

THE King of Hungary's daughter wanders
    down her garden green,
The roses hang in the apple boughs, the lilacs
    stand between.

She wanders singing to herself, at peace in the
    early day,
" Glory to God " she sings as clear as saints
    in Heaven may.

The King of Hungary's daughter wanders
    singing to the gate,
And there she hears an angry brawl that stops
    her singing straight.

" O what's the din at the gate, my lords ? "
    she passes through the door,
And there she sees a beggar man that's fallen
    to the floor.

All white above his blinded eyes an evil
    stripe goes round ;
The staff has fallen from his hands, he faints
    in a deathly swound.

There's not a knight i' the castle-yard but
    spurns the thing that moans,
A huddled stain of rags and wounds upon the
    whited stones.

There's not a squire i' the castle-yard but
    strikes his steely foot,
And points his jest at Lazarus that makes such
    humble suit.

" O knights, for the love of Christ who died,
    O gentle ladies all,
Is there none will give me a crust of bread, a
    stale crust and a small ? "

" There's other mouths for our crusts, beggar,
    there's dogs and hounds enow,
They bring us hares from hunting home, but
    thou—what bringest thou ? "

"O knights, there's a time to die, a time to
    sorrow, a time to jest.
Is there never a hole in all your barns where a
    man may die at rest?"

"How darest thou ask the boon, beggar, a
    plague upon thy pride!
What horse would lie in the straw, forsooth,
    whereon a leper died?"

The King of Hungary's daughter hears and
    reaches out her hand,
"Rise up, rise up, thou weary guest, an' thou'st
    the strength to stand.

"I'll lead thee to my chamber, there I'll set
    the meat and wine,
Thou shalt not lie in the horses' beds, thou'llt
    sleep more sound in mine."

She's ta'en the beggar by the hand; and all
    the courtiers stare,
"And what will the king say now?" they cry;
    "and what will a maiden dare?"

"And who shall tell the bonny prince that she
    is bound to wed?
How will he like a leper laid within his lady's
    bed?"

They're gone in gangs to spread the news,
    they whisper loud and sly:
The king and all those gentlemen to the
    maiden's chamber hie.

They burst the unlatchet door, and lo! they
    fall before the bed.
Then turned the king's young daughter: "And
    why do you kneel?" she said.

"There's nothing strange i' the room, I think,
    but the poor sick man you know,
You did not kneel i' the yard downstairs; why
    are you kneeling now?"

She looks at all the fainting knights with wide
    and wondering eyes,
She looks towards the bed whereon the Christ
    in glory lies.

But she, who sees the Christ in all that suffers,
    does not see
The awful splendour of His crown, the terror
    of Deity.

The knights are blind, they cannot breathe in
    that unearthly air :
The King of Hungary's daughter alone is
    unaware.

   Feb. 12, 1888.

Our Lady of the Broken Heart.

"*Love seeketh not itself to please,*
Nor for itself hath any care,
But for another gives its ease,
And builds a heaven in hell's despair."

BLAKE.

8

ACT I.

SCENE I. *An Italian Garden : a terrace ; to the left, an Arbour ; to the right, an Ilex-grove and Shrine.*

TIME. *Seventeenth Century, or any time.*

Hilarion [alone seated in an arbour, in the Public Garden].
And so my April-minded Bellamy
Is happy with my friend, and he with her.
'Tis well ; and yet 'tis pity ; for, alas,
I would not lose her yet, so young she is !
And 'tis a sudden fancy.   Scarce a month
Since either heard the other's voice at first
And started, thinking it a rarer music
Than they had known before.
                              Ah, Julian, Bellamy,
You are both happy ; but I happier,
Because in silence and without reward
I love the dearest woman in the world ;
Oh, worth a thousand sisters !

[*Hesperia passes.*]   Can it be !
O dream turned truth, change not in air again.
How long have I looked forward to this hour,
And dare not now believe my love-sick eyes
That see things all one colour.
    Hesp. [*coming nearer*].   Hilarion ?
    Hil.   Hesperia !   ('tis she !)

                        I am glad to meet you.
    Hesp.   Well met indeed !   My father, ailing lately,
And sightless now, you know, will second me
In welcomes to you.
    Hil.   It is very long
Since last I saw him.   Is he unwell?
    Hesp.   I fear
He never will be better this side Heaven.
And he is all I have !
    Hil.   Sigh not, dear lady.
I hope that he may live for many years ;
The old are long a-dying.
    Hesp.   He's far from well
I think his blindness creeps upon his spirit.
    Hil.   Yet grieve not ere the hour ; for Grief, being come,
Is less intolerable than is the dread

We have of it.   'Tis easy to be sad,
When sadness must be, and most natural.
It is the fear of Sorrow in happy hours
That eats the heart away and cankers life.

   Hesp.   Ay, you were ever melancholy !

   Hil.   I trust not.

I bring you remedies for melancholy.

   Hesp.   You're sad indeed, if such sad thoughts console you !
Have you no holier cures ?

   Hil.   None for myself.

For you that lovely are and well-beloved
I never hope to need one.

   Hesp.   Nay, I fear
You are unskilled in comfort, for indeed
My father's blind this year and dying now ;
And I, that sit all day and watch and dread
The terrible oncoming of the end.
I cannot mind to be considered fair
Who am not fortunate.

   Hil.   There is more love
I' the world than fathers give !

   Hesp.   But none thus sole
And treasurable.   Peace to my forebodings !

Poor welcome to an old friend newly met !

Tell me, how have you fared, Hilarion ?

Hil.   As ever in your absence—bearing life

With fortitude, I trust, but as a burden.

Hesp.   You are very courtly, sir !   I think you younger

By a month or so than I, who have out-grown

These compliments.   Come, tell me of the friends

We had at Pisa.   How is Frederic—Julian.

Hil.   The last is here with me.

Hesp.   What Julian here ?

Back from his home in England.   Julian here.

And I've not seen him !   Tell me, is he well,

Strong, happy ?

Hil.   Have we met at last, at last,

To speak of Julian ?   Tell me of yourself.

And we will talk and listen of old days

Together.

Hesp.   Nay, take care ; they are full of Julian !

Hil.   No matter so you speak.   Say anything !

Hesp.   Nay, it is you must talk.   I have no news.

Tell me, I pray, how come you here with Julian ?

I do suppose he thinks I am at Pisa,

And goes to find me there.

Hil.   To find you ?   Julian ?

Hesp.   Ay.   Did he never tell you of our secret ?
We were contracted ere he went to England,
A year ago when his old father died.
My father still was lecturer at Pisa,
And Julian ever was his favourite
Of all the students.   But I thought you knew
How our long friendship blazed to sudden love
At the ominous threat of parting.   Now I hope
The worst of that is over.

Hil.   I never knew it !
I do assure you, lady.   I never knew it !

Hesp.   Nay, nay, it is no matter !   I had thought
That Julian would have told you long ago.
But he is English, of a sterner make
Than we Italians.   Tell me now of Julian.

Hil. [*aside*].   O my sweet outraged sister.   O my heart,
What can I tell ?

          [*Aloud*].   I think they are false, these English.

Hesp.   Nay, sir.   I will not speak again with you.
'Tis you are false that are so courteous,
And yet so quick to blight an absent friend.
Take heed, take heed.   Nay, I will never scold ;

I give you a good-morrow ; my father calls me.

[*Exit Hesperia.*

Hil. [*alone*].   O my sweet sister !   O my broken heart !
And O Hesperia, wronged the most of all !
How has this triple traitor bound our lives
Into one cord of woe.   Bellamy ! Bellamy !
My little, childish, and so happy child,
Whom none has ever crossed in all the world,
Will you grow pale and die perhaps, or sicken
At heart with vague and maddening melancholy
When he shall marry my Hesperia ?
And yet, my sister, if he's true to you
He'll wrong the dearest woman in all the world,
And break her faithful heart.   O treacherous friend !
There is no way but misery out of this.
I can not save the nearest things I have
From certain sorrow.   Heaven, give me counsel,
And show me any way that saves them both,
Howe'er it break my heart.   O patience, patience !
Be quiet, hands, and feel not for the sword
That will not cut this knot.   Oh, I'll be patient,
For God wills all, and in His will is rest.
If ill be ours, content with ill is best !

SCENE II. *On the Terrace. Far off the sea.*

JULIAN *and* BELLAMY.

Bell. There sets the sun ! Look how the waters turn !
And see the moon—how large and white arising—
Leaps up the fiery sky !

Jul. So sudden Love,
When first I saw you, in my passionate heart,
Shone out and made it holy.

Bell. Still the moon,
Julian, is but a feeble luminary ;
And I am very jealous of the sun,
By whose remembered light I shine. What, silent ?
And did you never love before you saw me ?

Jul. Oft with my fancy, never with my heart.

Bell. Still, you *have* loved. I am sorry. See the sky
Is grown quite dark and frightened.

Jul. Courage, sweet.
'Twas but a cloud ; there shines the moon again
Like Love on sorrow.

Bell.   Then I'll be your moon.
I'll swear you told those other women all
And each, she was your sun—but none your moon
Merely ! Nay, frown not. . . . From the harbour's edge
The fishers push their boats sheer off to sea.
Listen, the plashing oars ! . . . Ah, there I heard
A word of the song they sing.   All day they rest,
They rest and waste the common golden hours ;
For with moon-rising their life's work begins.
Julian, I'll be your moon !   Or, if too little,
The pale, small evening star !

   Jul. (starting)   Nay, would you mock me ?
   Bell.   Love ?
   Jul.   Were I worthy of you, Bellamy !
My heart is a black night for you to shine in !
   Bell.   You come from talking with Hilarion
Surely ?   Why, that's the very trick of his tongue !
Nay, it is hard on me to be so taxed
With a merry heart and a melancholy lover.
Be cheered, because I know no way to cheer you—
I that was never clever !
   Jul.   Oh, forgive me.
   Bell.   You are forgiven, Sire, for being sad !
Why, here's the Arch-mourner—here's Hilarion,

My brother, whose one jest lies in his name—
(And that's as fit as a farce at a funeral !)
The chief Apostle of Misery !   He's in earnest.
Last week he laughed at lovers ; but on Thursday
You and I quarrelled, Julian ; and thereat,
From the strangeness of his speech, I do believe
He fell in love to be more miserable ;
But, silence.   Here he comes.

   Jul.   Good even, Hilarion.

   Bell.   This rose I'll give you for your thoughts, my brother.

   Hil.   I take your rose, and give you leave to guess them.

   Bell.   Oh !   How the sun's no great light after all
But a lantern riddled with the lucky shots
Of you philosophers.   Or how this rose
Is a pleasant bed for a cankerworm to lie in.
What reck I of your dreams ?

   Hil.   Not much, I think.
'Tis late, my little sister !

   Bell.   Well, good-night.
You would talk secrets with my Julian.
And so you cheer him better than I can.
I'll not be jealous.

    [*Turns, with a curtsey, to Julian, who stands apart musing.*
              So your moon retires.

Jul.   Good-night.

[*Exit Bellamy. Julian ánd Hilarion walk on together, silent.*
                            Suddenly.

Hil.   There Hesper shines !   Star of my lady, hail !—
Dearest of planets, shine and shame the moon
With holier beams !

          [*To Julian*]   Do you remember her ?

Jul.   Remember whom, thou high-fantastical lover ?

Hil.   The angel of my memory, Hesperia.

                                   [*A pause.*

What, will you pale to hear another praised
That is not Bellamy ?   Oh, lover's ardour !

Jul.   Nay, nothing ails.   Go on.

Hil. [*with scrutiny*].   But you are faint.

Jul.   Nothing—it is nothing !   Tell me of your lady.

Hil.   You know Sebastian the Humanist
Who lectured on philosophy at Pisa
In the University when we were there ?
After you left he went stone blind ; and then
He earned his bread by teaching for some while,
Earning much work, scant praise, and scanter bread.
But happily Hesperia his daughter——

Jul. [*aside*].   Hesperia.

Hil. [*markedly*].   You *must* remember her.

Jul. [*after a pause*].   Yes.   I remember—
A piece of sainted nature.

Hil.   I am glad
You say so.

Jul.   Yet I wonder that you love her.
I think I ever fancied her a creature
To pray to, not to love.

Hil.   Are you in earnest ?

Jul.   What do you mean ?

Hil.   Nothing—an idle question !

Jul.   'Tis true, I had a holy fancy for her
When we were boy and girl ; before I knew
How much less good, how very much less fair,
An angel is than a woman.

                          But I think
She has forgotten me, as I have her.
It is so long ago.

Hil.   I would make sure on't.

Jul.   I will ; but, prythee, tell me how she rescued
Her father at this pass.

Hil.   I am too glad
To have the chance to dwell upon her praises.

I do not think there is a better theme
In all the world, or any nobler service.
Well, in Sebastian's poverty she learned
All that the old man, dispossessed and blind,
Taught in his frequent leisure ; and so well,
That in a year she knew the curious types
Grown dark to him, could read, collect, survey
With patience and quick inference and love
Unwearied.

   Jul. [*impatiently*].   As your own is weariful—
When comes the point to this exordium
On female knowledge ?

   Hil.   Now : Hesperia,
Being grown, in fine, more sensible eyes to him
Than those he lost, the University
Proclaimed him Lecturer again. . . . When last
I saw Hesperia——

   Jul.   When ?   Where ?

   Hil. [*slowly*].   To-day !
[*a pause*] Julian, she is a very noble lady !
If any wronged her, I were wroth with him
Even to death.

   Jul.   Why do you tell me this?

Hil. I speak from a full heart—I love Hesperia,
And wish her well more than I wish myself:
More than I wish my little Bellamy,
(My sunshine and the eyes I see it with)
Who were with less content—

                  I love Hesperia !
Julian, in all this Heaven there are no stars
That shine so bright as Honour and Hesperia !

    Jul. I will not bear this rant !

                     What do you mean
With your veiled words and smooth Italian way?

    Hil. I only tell you of a noble lady
As sweet as any are that live in Heaven,
As true and patient as they were on earth.
I only say how dearly I do love her
(But only as a friend, an honest friend) ;
And how I would indeed avenge to death
A slight that any villain laid upon her.

    Jul. I like it not.

    Hil.   But since you are so dull
And callous of her praise, I say farewell t' you.
Have you a word, perchance, for Bellamy ?
I take her home to Pisa in the morning—

Jul.   Take Bellamy?

Hil.   Ay—and I leave Hesperia !
Nay, hast thou never loved, that thou must start
To hear the ravings of a lover's heart !   [*Exit Hilarion.*

Jul. [*alone*].   I do believe he has some plain suspicion
Of that most hasty and ill-omened contract
Which binds me to Hesperia.   Oh, I know
That such a bond is little less than marriage
In this fastidious Italy.   I know
That breaking it would blot Hesperia
And brush the glory from her aureole—
Must I then marry her ? that cold, pale beauty.
I do not love her now, I never loved her ;
And I do not believe she loved me either—
Surely I never loved, till Bellamy
With her sweet laughter and her girlish eyes
Stole in my heart.
                    O cold Hesperia !
To think of you is like the chill of death—
O hateful ghost !   I feel you take my hand
And slip your icy ring on its hot pulses,
And lead me far away from Bellamy—
Bellamy, I'll go sing to you, sweet Bellamy

They take away to-morrow.   One last song,
One last sweet music fraught with hope and dreams—
And then, I'll either see you never more—
Or win my longed-for freedom from Hesperia !   [*Exit Julian.*

SCENE III.   *The same night.*   HESPERIA *and* SEBASTIAN *in
an arbour.   Outside, under the shadow of a cypress hedge,*
JULIAN, *tuning and practising a mandoline.*

Hesp. [*reading aloud*].

" *Where walk the Nymphs, the Bacchanals ; where flows
The fount of Castaly—*"

                              Nay, 'tis not there—
(Some one is playing surely in the garden
Upon an instrument ?)   Oh, here's the line :

[*reads*] " *Now, since the city and its people sicken,
Come Thou with healing steps across the slopes
Of steep Parnassus, over thundering straits—*"

Father, I find the chorus difficult.
   Sebas.   Nay, girl, go on—'Tis very near the end.

9

Hesp.   Is that a mandoline they play outside?
[*reads*] "*O Thou, the Master of the Quire of stars,*
         The bright flame-breathing stars!   O Leader, thou
         Of all the voices that do sing by night,
         Deign to appear."
                              It *is* a mandoline !
Sebas.   What then ?
Hesp.   I know that air.
Sebas.   No doubt you know it.
Some tune the students sing o' nights in Pisa ;
Go on, I prithee, daughter.
Hesp. [*reads*].   "*O appear,*
         Thou Son of God, with following Naxian girls
         That in a maddening frenzy all night long
         Shall wildly dance to thee and wildly sing
         And call thee, Iacchus !"
                         Nay, I cannot, father.
I think there is some magic in the tune
They play in the garden there . . . I know it well.
    Sebas.   You are not used to stint me in your reading
To please your idler fancy.
    Hesp. [*kneeling at his side and taking his hands*].
                         Forgive me, father !
I am not well. . . . I have heard news to-day . . .

I have heard news to-day that stirs me strangely—
Ay, news of Julian !

    Sebas.   Has he come to take you ?
'Tis well you teach me to give up your voice.
Let your eyes shut for me—be dark again—
So you will go to England?

    Hesp.   Patience, father. !.
Oh, I will never leave you till I die ;
If one, or you or Julian, be mine,
And only one, I shall know how to choose !
You are my father, and you are alone ;
You gave me even the very heart I love with.
[*She rises up*] But Julian ever was your favourite,
And you will gain a son !

    Sebas.   I was not blind then :.
I did not fear so much to lose a daughter.
To rob my heart and shut its bird away
In a green nest afloat on misty seas,
So far, too far, where I can never come—
But tell me what you heard ?

    Hesp. [*goes to stand in the doorway*].   Oh, all the night
Is full of hope and strange mysterious beauty.
The moon that rides so ample in the skies·
Sends down a flood of light upon the roses:
That smell less sweet by day

Sebas.   So, it is fine, then?

Hesp.   Ay, finer than it ever was before,
When Paris and Œnone walked alone
On Ida . . . Oh, my father, Julian's here !

Sebas.   Here? Where? You are very strange to-night,
    Hesperia !

Hesp.   Ay, strange to miss the empty absent ache
And sense of loneliness.   That word is dead—
Oh, fallen from my language now !

                                 Nay, father,
Nay, look not pale !   I am a cruel daughter—
I am unkind, I know ; but never lonely—
I love you more than any other father
Ever was loved in Italy !

Sebas.   Nay, patience—
Why you are weeping, child !

Hesp.   O 'tis for joy—
Father, there is a firefly in the shade
Of that aspiring cypress.   All this time
It has looked green and faint, and poised as still
As it was held there by invisible strings ;
But, on a sudden, loosed, I know not how—
It floats up now, up, up, to join the stars,
With an unsteady, circling, wavering motion,

No longer green, but gold against the blue
It goes to seek.   I think my heart is loosed
Like that, and floats so dizzily heavenwards.

    Sebas.   I do not understand you !

    Hesp.   Oh, hush.   The music !

    Jul. [*trying his mandoline outside.   Sings*].
        Were you a star
                Above,
      Shining too far
                for Love ;
      Yet were I glad,
                Though you rode so above me,
      Dreaming my star
                Did she know me would love me !
      Now am I sad !

    Hesp. [*aside*].   Earth swerves beneath.   His singing thrills
    the night
With passion.   Stars turn giddy at his voice !

    Jul. [*sings*].
        Were you a pearl,
                Below
      Stir of the whirl
                and flow,

> *Drowned in the deep,*
>> *Yet a spirit could show me,*
> *Hope that my pearl*
>> *Would be mine did she know me.*
> *Now must I weep!*

Hesp. [*still aside*].   Not if thou knewest my heart!   Each
fibre's thine!

Now at the top of bliss, I thank thee God,

Ensue what may, that thou hast given me life.

Jul. [*sings*].

> *Light of my heart,*
>> *My Dream,*
> *Little apart*
>> *We seem ;*
> *Nearer the sky*
>> *To the sea's lowest stream is*
> *Than to my heart*
>> *My delight and my dream is!*
> *Well may I sigh.*

Hesp. [*aloud*].   No more!   No more!   Adieu, concealing
shame,

And try no more that true and faithful heart.

Julian, my lover, take me, I am thine.

> [*Steps from the arbour's hedge.*

Jul. [*steps forward*].   Lady Hesperia !

Hesp.   Oh, it is my Julian !

                                                    [*Swoons.*

SCENE IV.   *Early morning. . . An Ilex grove and shrine*
                with withered garlands.

Hesp. [*alone*].   For still it seems to me impossible
That while I thus remember, he forgets ;
And yet there was a coldness in his voice,
Or else I fancied it.

                        Oh, it was fancy !
For I believe it ever must be thus
After so long a parting . . . there's a gulf
Of absence lies between us.

                                [She approaches the shrine.
                        It is here
That he will meet me in a little hour.
How grey the shadow lies, the ilex-shadow
That always looks like death ! . . . The valley sleeps
In blue and filmy quiet. . . . It is morning,
Less passionate than night.

                        [She leans her arms on the ledge of the shrine.

O sad Madonna,
O pierced at heart with seven cruel swords,
There is a sharper sword that never pricked you
With shrewd suspicion of the thing you love . . .
Too base Hesperia !

> [*She sits down on a stone at the side of the shrine.*

(A girl's voice outside is heard singing :)
> " *Strow poppy buds about my quiet head,*
>   *And pansies on mine eyes . . .* "

Hesp.   Some poor soul goes singing
Her song o' the swan ! some girl who's lost her lover,
While I have mine again alive and true . . .
O Julian, I will nevermore suspect
Your truth, that is less tender than the phantom
I made of womanish dreams to fill your place
In absence with the memory of your smile !

> *(The voice comes nearer :)*
> " *Strow poppy buds about my quiet head,*
>   *And pansies on mine eyes,*
>   *And rose leaves on the lips that were so red,*
>   *Before they blanched with sighs.*"

Hesp.   Sweet singing !   How might I have been like her,
And am not.   O poor soul, she is very sad !

(*Voice still nearer:*)

" *Let gillyflowers breathe their fragrant breath*
   Under my tired feet ;
But do'not mock the heart that starved to death
   With aught of fresh or sweet."

Hesp.   Lo, here she comes ; she is young, and fair, and gentle,
But crazed with grief, I fear.

Enter BELLAMY, *pale and dishevelled, boughs of rose and acacia
in her arms.*

Bell.   I know the maidens
Bring her more garlands than the other Virgins
Through all the month of May ; but it is June,
And see, their boughs are withered and their blooms.
But I bring more, I think, than any other
Ever has brought before. . . . 'Tis sure she'll hear me !

                 [*She lets fall the heap of branches.*

O Virgin, whom the sorrowing country people
Do call Madonna of the Broken Heart,
Heal mine a cruel brother broke this morning
And keep me safe, and hide me whom they seek
To take away from a most virtuous lover.
Thou pitying Mother-maid !

     [*She kneels down and sees Hesperia sitting under the shrine.*

Are you an Angel ?

Or who are you that sit so cool and sweet

Under the shadow of the Virgin's shrine ?

   Hesp.   Fear not, my flower, for I would never harm you,

I only am a maiden like yourself

And fain would help you.

   Bell.   Oh, I know you now !

Divine Madonna, are you come to help me ?

   Hesp.   Nay, child. . . .

   Bell.   O Virgin, see, I came to seek you.

See, when the mists were heavy on the garden,

While still the dawn was grey, I stole and plucked

These crimson roses, and these yellow roses,

And these pink delicate roses that run wild ;

And all this wealth of heavy-sweet acacia,

To honour you and die before your shrine. . . .

See how my hands are torn. . . . Ay, and my heart, too.

I pray you heal it !

   Hesp.   Thou poor child !

   Bell.   I knew not

The Virgin used to wander in the woods

About her shrine. . . . I did not hope to find you,

Save in a painted image. . . . I'd not ventured

Knowing that I should find you sitting silent

Alone upon the hills.

Hesp.   O sweet, you wander.
I am not what you think !
   Bell.   And will you help me ?
   Hesp.   Sure, if I can.
   Bell.   Then, prithee, help me soon,
For I am sick at heart, and yesternight
I was so happy !   Then Hilarion. . . .
   Hesp.   Hilarion ?
   Bell.   He is my cruel brother
Who ever was most tender till last night.
He was my father and my mother too,
And held my orphan baby hands in his
When first I tried to walk.   And oh, I loved him.
But now he's cruel.
   Hesp.   Nay, I do not think so.
   Bell.   Indeed he is ; he came to me last night,
And solemnly he bade me pray to Heaven
I might not even dream o' nights of Julian
But quite forget him.
   Hesp.   ·   Julian !
   Bell.   Ay, my lover.
Virgin you know all this, and still I tell you,
I am so sick at heart.
   Hesp.   For Julian ?

Bell.   Ay.
Nay, frown not, Holy Mother, look not strange
And angry on me, or I shall go mad ;
You are my only hope.   O never spurn me,
Thou Mother of the afflicted !
Hesp.   Do not rave so.
There is more quiet in a broken heart.
Bell.   Oh, well I know you have had worse to bear,
But you are sainted, and you are Madonna,
And have another heart to bear it with. . . .
It is for that you can so well console us,
O Mary, mother of the miserable,
Because your heart still bleeds. . . .

                            But I am weak,
Little and earthly, and I should go mad,
Wicked, and kill myself to feel such sorrow.
Hesp.   Ay, is it so ?
Bell.   It is, indeed.
Hesp.   I feared it.
Bell.   And so, indeed, sweet Virgin, you must help me.
Hesp.   I cannot let you die.
Bell.   Madonna !
Hesp.   Hush !
O sweet, be still. . . . I cannot bear your voice, yet.

Bell. True, I would fain be still or else more happy. . . .
I pray you, Virgin, give me Julian back,
Or else lay down my head upon your heart,
And take my hands within your heavenly hands ;
I'll shut my lids and you shall breathe upon them,
Once, softly, with your cold unearthly breath.
And I will wake with you in Paradise.

   Hesp. Nay, maiden.

   Bell.   Leave me not.

   Hesp.   Nay, sweet, be quiet.

        [She draws a curious ring from her hand, slowly.

   [Aside].   O little ring, O fraught with memories,
How have I kissed his ancient kisses from thee.
I must not do it more.

   [To Bellamy].   Give me your hand.

   Bell. Is this the seal of death ? I am not frightened.

   Hesp. Nay, little maid : it is the seal of Love,
Of youth, and happy love, and tender hopes,
Of all that maidens dream of in the night,
When through their open window steals a breath
Of roses warm in June, or lover's music. . . .
(That music was for you.) . . . But I must go
Back to my emptied life and leave you here.

         [She stoops and kisses Bellamy.

Lie still among your flowers, and pray awhile,
Till Julian come ; then give him back the kiss
I gave you. Ah, God ! . . . Show him the ring. . . .
And he will know your secret.

> *[She moves to go but turns back.*
> For Hilarion.

Love him most truly ; he is very noble.

Bell.   And must you leave me, ever dear Madonna ?

Hesp.   I must.

Bell.   My love and dearest thanks attend you.

> *[Exit Hesperia, as from the other side Julian enters.*

Jul.   This was the place ; now, courage !

[he discovers Bellamy.]   Bellamy ?

Bell.   Julian

> *[They embrace.*

1878–1886.

FINIS.

UNWIN BROTHERS, THE GRESHAM PRESS, CHILWORTH AND LONDON.

RETURN
TO → **CIRCULATION DEPARTMENT**
202 Main Library

LOAN PERIOD 1	2	3
HOME USE		
4	5	6

ALL BOOKS MAY BE RECALLED AFTER 7 DAYS

Renewals and Recharges may be made 4 days prior to the due date.

Books may be Renewed by calling 642-3405.

DUE AS STAMPED BELOW